GOOD KNIGHT, BAD KNIGHT

TOM KNIGHT

t

templar publishing

The summer was over
and it was time to go back to school.

Bad Knight hated school.

The teachers were too strict.

The work was too difficult.

And all the other kids made fun of him.

"Wow, you really ARE a bad knight,"
they said.

But this year was going to be different.
Bad Knight was building a secret weapon.

He was going to show everyone
what he was really capable of.

What's more, Bad Knight's cousin was coming to stay.
With his help, Bad Knight would show the kingdom
he was a truly GREAT knight.

But when his cousin arrived, Bad Knight quickly realised that he was not what he'd expected.

This was terrible!
Bad Knight's cousin was GOOD!

Things were even worse at school.
Good Knight was top of the class in everything.

Maiden rescuing . . .

. . . swordsmanship . . .

. . . archery . . .

. . . and even tapestry making.

Good Knight
Clever Knight
Sporty Knight
Fun Knight
Happy Knight
Friendly Knight
Tired Knight
Lazy Knight
Wheezy Knight
Bad Knight

By the time the final exams came around, Bad Knight was officially the worst knight in school. What's more, the worst knight had to face the best knight at the end-of-term jousting match.

And guess who the best knight was?

The day of the big tournament dawned.

Bad Knight pulled down his visor and
prepared himself for the worst.

POW!

The worst came very quickly.

Good Knight had won!
The crowd went wild.

But Bad Knight had
spotted something
in the sky.

It was an ENORMOUS dragon, and it was heading straight for Good Knight!

Suddenly, Bad Knight knew exactly what to do.
Flapping his arms in the air, he led the dragon away from his cousin.

Bad Knight's plan had worked.
The dragon was heading straight for him.

Using his catapult,
Bad Knight fired his brand
new troll-breath stink bomb
straight at the dragon's
gaping mouth.

The whole school erupted into cheers as the dragon queasily flew back to where it had come from. Bad Knight had saved the day!

He was dubbed BEST Knight in School.

Everyone was very proud of Bad Knight, especially Good Knight.

The two boys were inseparable for the rest of Good Knight's visit.
Together they figured out new maiden-rescuing techniques.

They worked on their
swordsmanship skills . . .

. . . and practised archery together.

Bad Knight even started to enjoy tapestry making.

And they finally perfected the catapult and made it
even better than it was before . . .

. . . because maybe they really weren't
that different after all.